Candlelight and Pancakes

Susan Mellon

Candlelight and Pancakes

First Print Edition: December 2019

Editing: Precision Editing Group
Cover: Brenda Walter
Formatting: Blue Valley Author Services
ISBN: 9781705336373

TABLE OF CONTENTS

CHAPTER 1

MELODY TOSSED HER SUITCASE CARELESSLY on top of her bed. She was done. She needed to get away for a weekend by herself. Away from all the couples in love. Away from all the red hearts and glitter that hung in every store window. Away from the greeting cards for people to profess their love for one another. And away from every restaurant that only took reservations for couples on February 14. Valentine's Day was Melody's favorite holiday while growing up. So much so, that people would tell her she had an old soul trapped in a young body. She was a hopeless romantic, and it showed. She loved reading a good romance novel and watching romantic movies. She loved everything lace and all things pastel colored.

Melody's mind drifted back to her fifth-grade Valentine's Day party at school. The class spent the weeks leading up to it constructing and decorating homemade boxes. The students would use the boxes to collect valentines from their classmates. She had made hers from an old cardboard shoe box and carefully wrapped it in red paper. Then she glued paper hearts on it, topping it off with a sprinkle of glitter.

She'd loved receiving those little cards and being asked to be someone's Valentine. There were puppies and kittens, trucks, and silly-looking creatures with googly eyes all requesting the same sentiment of "be mine." The night before the party she had spent hours making her valentines. She had to make sure the right classmate was matched with the right affection. Carefully, she had printed their names on each envelope using colored pens. Looking back on that now, it was no wonder she had become a marketing executive for a greeting card company.

Scouring the internet for country B-&-Bs that weren't already booked was no easy task. Especially last minute. This was Wednesday, and Valentine's Day was on Saturday. Melody was lucky that her boss let her take time off work last minute. She needed a reservation for three nights. Page after page of B-&-Bs and inns offered the same results. Booked. Just as Melody was about to give up, she stumbled across the Sugar & Spice Inn.

Pulling her phone from the back pocket of her jeans, she quickly punched the numbers in. The familiar sound of beep ... beep ... beep resonated in her ear. Tossing the phone on her bed, she reached for her laptop. She maneuvered around the website and made a reservation online for the next three nights. Turning her computer off, she shoved it aside. She pulled her suitcase to the edge of the bed, sat down beside it, and unzipped the zipper.

Melody decided to call her sister, Gabby. The phone rang several times before Gabby answered.

"Mel!" the cheerful voice sounded.

"Gabby, I have you on speaker. I'm packing."

"For what?"

"I'm leaving tomorrow. I have reservations."

"Now? Do you think that's wise?" Gabby asked, sounding a bit concerned.

"Always being the big sister," Melody chimed, shaking her head. Folding three pair of blue jeans, she laid them in the bottom of the suitcase. Just because she was eighteen months older, Gabby thought that gave her the right to interfere into Melody's business all the time. Whether she was asked or not. Melody pulled three sweaters and a parka from her closet, adding them to the suitcase.

"You do realize we are expecting several inches of snow this weekend?" Gabby sighed, loud enough for her sister to hear. "Not the best time to take off on a whim."

"It's not a whim." She rolled her eyes. She hated lying to Gabby. Melody's reservation was a spur-of-the-moment decision. It was the only way to keep Gabby off her back. "I've been planning this for a while. I am headed to the Sugar and Spice Inn in Williamsport."

"Williamsport? That's four hours from Pittsburgh."

"Not a big deal, sis. I'm just going to hop on Interstate 80, and I'll be there in no time. Anyway,

I didn't call so you can play mother hen. I need you to check on Holly for me while I'm away. I'll be back on Sunday."

"Sure, providing we aren't snowed in! Put extra water and food out for her, just in case."

"Thank you!" She ended the call before the questions started.

Holly jumped onto the bed, stretching her legs, one at a time, making sure she was seen. Melody pulled the zipper shut. Picking Holly up, she scratched her behind her ears. "Sisters!" The white-and-gray striped cat purred.

Melody put her suitcase on the passenger seat next to her. She slipped off her coat, laying it across her suitcase. She hated driving in a winter coat. It made her feel confined. She hated being stuck in small spaces. When she was five years old, she had gotten stuck inside an old steam trunk that belonged to her parents. She and Gabby always played hide-and-seek with their dad. Every day after work, at 5:15 p.m. on the nose he'd be home. She and her sister would hide from him. Usually, their giggling and shushing each other revealed where they were hiding.

Then it happened. They always hid together, but one day they decided not to. Gabby crawled under their parents' bed, and Melody had run to the basement. She'd hid in an old trunk. She didn't know the latch was broken. She'd climbed in and pulled the lid shut. Melody had been stuck inside for several hours, until finally a locksmith was able to get her out. Her dad had drilled holes in the trunk while she was stuck, so she'd been fine. But after that experience she'd never played hide-and-seek again.

Setting her mug of hot chocolate in the cup holder, Melody synced her phone with her car's bluetooth and started listening to the audio book she'd downloaded: "The Fragrance of Love." She was set. The sun was bright, the air was crisp, and not a snowflake to be seen. Starting the ignition, she shouted above the audio book, "Farewell, Valentine's Day!"

By the time she reached I-80 the snow had started. First it started falling slowly, dancing and swirling through the air, announcing its presence. Not settling, just fluttering about. The closer she got to Williamsport, the heavier the snow became. Instead of just fluttering in the air, it now looked more like a white curtain that was steadily coming down. Melody turned her wipers on to the constant mode and slowed a bit. *I hate it when Gabby's right.*

She had planned on stopping for dinner at the Stonehouse Wood Fired Pizza and Pasteria but decided against it. She would eat at the inn once she got there. She shifted her RAV4 into four-wheel drive. Several inches of snow covered the road by now, and the cars on the road slowed to a crawl. The snow was becoming more aggressive and showed no signs of letting up.

Melody's four-hour drive turned into six, and it was beginning to get dark. Finally, she saw the turn-off for the inn. It was almost covered over by the snow, and the road was long and winding. There were no other houses or businesses on either side of the road. Both sides of the lane were lined with woods. She clicked on her map app. No signal showed this far into the woods. *Just great*, she thought. *I pay hundreds of dollars to have an updated phone and no signal.*

The snow was blowing straight into her windshield and felt hypnotic. She began to feel her eyes grow heavy and quickly rolled her window down a bit, letting the cold air rush in. She continued another ten minutes to the end of the road. A sign was posted in front of the inn, but the words were covered with snow.

"This has to be it," she spoke out loud. She wasn't sure, but even if she'd somehow missed her turn, she would plan on spending the night here. Hopefully. It'd be better than driving in the dark and the snow.

As she stepped into the snow her feet sank. The snow covered her ankles. Reaching across the seat, she grabbed her coat and suitcase. Then she climbed the steps to the porch, stomping her boots to release the snow that covered them. She rushed inside to get out of the cold.

The entryway had a raised desk that was located next to the stairs. She tossed her coat on the banister and set her suitcase near the steps. Glancing around, she called out. "Hello! Anyone here?"

A David Muir-look-alike appeared at the top of the steps. He paused for a second, peering down at her. He strutted down the steps with ease, stopping near Melody. He had perfect posture, with brown hair and eyes, and looked like he hadn't shaved in a couple days. She could see the whiskers forming along his square jaw. He was a little taller than she and wore blue jeans with a red, plaid flannel shirt. She looked at him from his head to his toes. He wasn't wearing shoes but instead wore a pair of dark-gray wool socks.

"I'm here!" she announced, trying to sound cheerful. She wasn't. She was tired and hungry. It had been stressful driving through the snow. She smiled and chuckled to herself. Standing next to her, the man resembled David Muir less. He was a bit shorter and not as lean. Perhaps he could pass as Muir's brother, if he had one.

"I can see that, but … who are you, and what are you doing here?"

CHAPTER 2

ZANDER LOOKED AT THE WOMAN standing in the entryway. She sounded so sure she was supposed to be there. Her coat was tossed on the banister as if it was a natural occurrence. Her long, brown hair cascaded, stopping at her shoulder blades, and her eyes were the shade of cedar. Even while wearing boots that had a wedge heel, the woman was a bit shorter than he.

She blinked a few times. “I’m Melody Chambers. I made reservations at your inn.”

“No, you didn’t,” he answered, matter-of-factly.

“Excuse me? Please don’t tell me you’re full?”

Zander chuckled. “I’m definitely not filled up, that’s for sure.”

“That’s a relief,” she sighed, resting one of her elbows on the desk. “I’m really tired. If you can just tell me what room I’m in ...”

“That’s what I’ve been trying to tell you. You don’t have a room here.” Zander watched as a look of bewilderment washed over her face.

"I don't understand. This is the Sugar Plum Inn, isn't it?"

"No. Yes." Zander shoved his hands into the front pockets of his jeans and walked around the desk, standing behind it. "The phone lines have been down for a few days, so you couldn't have made reservations."

"That explains why I got a busy signal when I called."

"Like I said ..."

"If I can just use your computer, I will show you the reservation I made. I reserved my room on your website."

"My what?" Whoever this lady was, she didn't make a reservation online. The inn didn't have a website. Staring at her, he could plainly see her look of determination.

"Your computer, laptop, or tablet. I will log in and show you the reservation I made. It's for tonight, Friday, and Saturday night."

"Look, miss, I don't own a computer, and Sugar Plum Inn certainly doesn't have a website. You must be mistaken."

"I'm not. And I left my laptop at home. I wanted to get away from it all ... including electronics." Melody took a deep breath and slowly exhaled. "I know," she said, pulling her cell phone from her purse. "I'll show you on my phone." She looked at it for a second and shoved it back into her purse. "No signal, great."

"Obviously, there's been some sort of mistake." Zander walked around the desk and took her coat and suitcase, extending them in her direction. That was when he noticed her lips. They were the color of apricots and had a natural pout to them. He liked that. "I'm sure you can find another place to stay."

Melody shook her head, taking her things from him. "Everything is booked solid for Valentine's weekend, plus there's a blizzard going on outside."

Zander looked at her with one raised eyebrow and walked toward the door. Surely she was exaggerating. Opening the door, he stepped onto the porch. Everything was covered in snow, and it was still falling. The snow illuminated the night like white, glistening dust. The trees that surrounded the inn sagged under its weight, almost as if they were bowing at his presence.

Zander turned and went back inside. "There must be six inches of snow out there, and it's still coming down." *Now what am I supposed to do?* He ran his fingers through his thick, brown hair. He looked at the stranger standing in the entryway. She was convinced she had made reservations at the inn. He certainly couldn't turn her away. Not while there was a blizzard brewing on the other side of the door. He watched as she pushed a few strands of her long, brown hair behind her ears. Her eyes seemed to catch every fleck of light, which made them sparkle.

"I'm Zander," he sighed. "And I guess you're spending the night, Miss Chambers. Follow me."

"Three." She corrected him.

"What?" he took the suitcase from her hands.

"Nights. The reservation is for three nights," she insisted.

Choosing to ignore her last statement, he climbed the steps.

Melody followed the man up the steps. Each step creaked beneath them, almost as if they were protesting. Melody envisioned the many guests that had stayed at the inn over the years. They'd walked up and down the very steps she was now using. She wondered briefly about those other people's stories.

At the top of the steps there was a small hallway, plainly decorated, with a hardwood floor that spilled over into each of the three guest rooms.

Zander flipped the light on in the first room at the top of the stairs. He set her suitcase on the floor, next to the bed.

Melody glanced around the small room. There was a full bed that filled the middle of the room, dressed in a lavender floral comforter with matching curtains on the windows. A small, plush green throw rug lay on the floor beside the bed. It offered a sanctuary of warmth, for bare toes against the cold hardwood flooring. A simple nightstand stood next to the bed and a chest of drawers along the wall. One picture hung on the wall above the small dresser. It was of the Sugar Plum Fairy from the ballet The Nutcracker.

"There's only one bathroom," Zander added, pointing across the hallway. "There's a linen closet in there with towels and such."

"Oh! Just one bathroom?" Melody grimaced at the idea of having to share a bathroom with strangers. That was something the website didn't mention. The very thought of that made her crinkle her nose with discontentment. She liked her privacy and savored lengthy, hot showers. Something she was sure she wouldn't be able to partake in if there was a line of people waiting outside the door. She hadn't noticed any other guests, though. She couldn't make up her mind if that was a blessing or not.

"Yep, that's it," he said. "Nothing fancy here."

"Okay then," she sighed. "I'm guessing I missed dinner?"

"Look, I'm not a cook."

She looked at Zander. He still hadn't moved from the doorway. If he was trying to make a statement that she was bothering him, he was succeeding. "I'm fine, really. I'll just get settled and see what I can scrounge up."

"Suit yourself," Zander replied, and left, closing the door behind him.

Melody sat on the edge of the bed, scrunching her nose. This was not exactly how she had imagined the Sugar Plum Inn to be like, and Zander wasn't anything how she imagined the owner of the inn to be. In fact, with the name like Sugar Plum Inn, she had expected an older woman to be running the place. A Mrs. Claus, if you will. Older, fat, and jolly, with a contagious laugh. Instead, the owner was a man. A young man, at that. The picture portrayed on the website looked warm and inviting. The picture was taken in the evening, and each windowsill boasted a lit candle. The porch was covered with flowers and plants, along with Adirondack and rocking chairs to relax on. Of course, the picture was taken in the summer and this was the dead of winter.

The one thing she did notice was that the inn was not inundated with Valentine's Day decorations. After all, that was what she was trying to escape this year. This was the first year she would not let herself romanticize about February 14. Her job did not make that an easy task. This was one of the biggest holidays of the year for her company.

She began unpacking. As she unzipped her suitcase she let her mind wander to her sister, Gabby. She had meant well fixing Melody up with Dillon. She wanted her to have what she had. Gabby was happily married and pregnant with her first baby. Her sister only wanted the same things for Melody. Perhaps too much. Melody knew her sister just wanted her to be happy. But after dating Dillon for six months, the two of them had amicably ended their relationship.

The wind outside blew across the windows, making them rattle. She crossed the room, pulling the curtains back. Looking outside, she could tell the snow was falling harder than it had been earlier. Of all the times for a snowstorm to happen. At least she was tucked away safe in the inn. Glancing at her phone, she saw that she still didn't have a signal. She could just picture her sister going crazy with worry about her.

CHAPTER 3

FINDING HER WAY TO THE kitchen, she turned the lights on. The kitchen was large, with a huge wooden table in the center. The table was big enough to serve ten people at one sitting. Melody let her hand glide across the top of it. It looked like a one-of-a-kind homemade piece. In the center of the table sat brass candlesticks with purple, taper candles protruding from the top.

A modest refrigerator stood in the corner of the kitchen. Opening the doors, Melody quickly scanned the contents for something to eat. There was a plate of leftover fried chicken. Grabbing two drumsticks, she closed the door. A hutch with shelving that matched the table, sat next to the refrigerator. Melody reached up, retrieving one of the country-patterned plates stacked there, and set it on the counter. Snatching a biscuit from the basket that sat on the counter, she put it on her plate and sat down at the huge table.

Just as she took a bite of chicken Zander walked in. "I see you found something to eat."

"I hope you don't mind." She swallowed the mouthful of chicken. "For someone who doesn't cook, this is pretty good." She looked at him, offering a small smile to break the ice.

"I didn't say I don't cook. I said ... I'm not a cook."

"You know, Zander, for an inn keeper, you aren't very friendly." She stood, taking her empty plate to the sink rinsing it off. Drying it, she put it on the shelf with the rest of the dinnerware. She could feel his eyes on her with every step she took. Watching her every move carefully. She turned and looked him square in the eyes. "I think I'll turn in now."

"Have it your way." Zander grabbed his coat from the hook next to the back door. "I'm going outside to the wood pile. The snow is still coming down. If we lose power like we did the phone lines, I'll make a fire."

Melody shrugged at Zander. "Have it your way," she mocked and strolled from the kitchen.

Pausing at the front desk, she casually flipped through the sign-in book. She found it odd that no one else was staying at the inn, especially this weekend. This was deemed the most romantic weekend of the year, at least by retail. Excluding herself, no one had stayed at the Sugar Plum Inn ... ever.

Looking up, she stared at the picture hanging on the wall behind the desk. It was of an older woman. She had curly hair and wore big, hoop-style earrings. The picture was taken in black-and-white, so Melody couldn't make out the color of the woman's hair or eyes, but she wore a blouse with huge polka-dots scattered across it and boasted a wide smile. Melody could even see a big piece of bubblegum smashed between her teeth.

Zander walked around the corner and stood for a second or two before speaking.

"That's Tulu," he offered, before she asked.

"Tulu?"

"Yes. She used to own this place."

"And she sold it to you?"

"Something like that." Zander yawned, stretching his arms out. "I'm hitting the sack. It's been a long day, with an unsuspecting turn of events thrown into the mix."

"You mean, me?"

"Yep, along with almost a foot of snow."

"I wish my phone had a signal, Zander, and I could show you the reservation I made."

"We'll figure it out later," he mumbled.

Melody watched him take the steps two at a time. The jeans he wore moved effortlessly with his stride.

The following morning Melody slipped into her robe and collected a few toiletries for her shower. She reached for the doorknob of the bathroom door just as Zander came out. His hair was still wet but combed back. He had on a thick, dark-green bathrobe that hung open in the chest area. Her eyes fell to the opening that revealed his chest and lingered for a few seconds.

"Good morning." She cleared her throat, forcing her gaze upward.

"Morning." Zander cracked a smile.

Melody squeezed passed him, closed the door, and latched the lock. Turning, she laid her items on the chair that was next to the sink and stopped in her tracks. Her eyes widened at the sight before her. There was no shower. A huge oval, clawfoot tub sat along the wall. Melody wiped her eyes and walked closer to the monstrosity. It had a mosaic, nickel-plated pattern across the outside of the tub, with copper feet and copper hardware.

"This can't be happening!" Melody deflated. Shaking her head, she sat on the chair. She crossed her legs and rested her head in her hands. She hated baths.

After glaring at the bathtub for a minute or two, she let out a groan of disappointment, stood, and flipped the hot water on, filling the tub. She'd entered the world of prehistoric.

She turned off the faucet and slipped out of her robe, letting it fall, surrounding her feet in a pool of satin. Then she dipped her red-painted toe into the water to gauge the temperature and lowered herself into the tub.

She washed quickly. She hated baths. She longed to feel hot water cascading over her from a hot shower. Her mind drifted to her encounter with Zander a few minutes ago. She was certain he noticed her looking at his chest. She couldn't help herself. His robe hung open.

Reaching with her toes, she pulled the plug and watched the water begin to lower. Stepping out of the tub, she grabbed her towel right away. Had it been this cold in the bathroom before her bath? Swiftly she dried and slipped back into her robe. She stood at the white, pedestal sink and looked in the round mirror that hung above it.

Pulling her hair, she piled it on top of her head and secured with an ivory clasp. Then she skirted to the door and flung it open. Rushing across the hall to her room, she nearly ran right into Zander. He had just come from the flight of steps that led to the attic.

He took hold of her shoulders instinctively. “Easy, easy. Where’s the fire?”

She looked at him and shivered. She wasn’t sure if she shivered from being cold or from the feel of his hands on her shoulders. “It’s cold in there.” She flung her free hand toward the bathroom.

“Is that all?” he released her.

“Is that all? I think you lost power.”

“Nope. No heat in the bathroom. Didn’t I mention that before?”

“What?” Melody shrieked. “No, you didn’t mention that.” She liked the way his hands felt on her shoulders. That fact irritated her. “It would’ve been nice, if you had.”

“Sorry. I don’t concern myself with little things like that, so it never occurred to me to say anything.”

“Little things! Heat is not a little thing, Zander.” She waited for some type of reaction. None came.

"Speaking of that, who doesn't have a shower? There's only a tub."

"Miss Chambers, I am fully aware of what's in the bathroom. I installed it myself."

"You mean, you did that on purpose?" she shifted her bare feet against the cold floor.

"Nice, isn't it?" Zander smiled.

Melody rolled her eyes. Now he smiles, and over a bathtub. He was a hard man to read. "I much prefer showers to baths."

"I could guess that." He turned to go down the steps but stopped and looked back at Melody. "I know your type." Then he was gone, disappearing down the stairs before she could reply to his comment.

"He knows my type," she huffed to herself as she went into her room to dress. He knew nothing about her.

CHAPTER 4

MELODY PAUSED IN THE LIVING room before going into the kitchen. It looked warm and inviting. There were two oversized suede couches, with a huge wooden coffee table between them. The coffee table was square and stained the same color as the kitchen table. The pieces of furniture looked like a matching set. The couches stood near a stone fireplace. A bay window sat along the front of the room, boasting a window seat loaded with pillows.

Walking closer to the mantel, she noticed a singular picture frame lying face down on it. She picked up the frame, revealing a photograph of a woman. If Melody had to guess, the woman was about the same age as she. The woman had short brown hair and a beautiful smile. Melody wondered who she was and laid the picture back the way she found it.

His guest walked into the kitchen as he was beginning to sip his coffee.

"Mmm." Melody took a deep breath. "Coffee smells good."

"Help yourself." Zander reached behind him, grabbing a cup and extending it toward Melody. He watched as she took the mug and filled it with the java. Her hair was pulled into a loose ponytail behind her head, and she wore leggings and boots with a long, black sweater that came to mid-thigh. He watched as she put the cup to her lips. "What size are you?"

Melody choked on her coffee, setting the cup back on the counter. "Excuse me?" she muttered through her coughing.

"What size are you?" he repeated. "Pretty simple question."

"That's none of your business!" her eyes widened.

"Look, it's not because I'm interested or anything like that." Zander rolled his eyes. "We have a situation that needs to be addressed."

"What situation?"

"It's still snowing, and the wind has picked up."

"And?" Melody asked.

"And the vents in the attic need to be covered. The cold air and snow are coming in."

"So, cover them." She reached for her coffee again.

"I can't fit, or I would."

"Can't fit where?"

"In the crawl space that leads to the gable vents." Zander turned his back toward Melody and set his cup in the sink. "That's what I need you to do." He turned back and looked at her. Melody's face seemed to move in slow motion as she registered what he had just said. Then it crinkled in way he'd never seen anyone do before.

"Nope, no way, Zander." She set her cup back on the counter again with a loud thud. "No, no, and let me see, no!"

"What? Why not? I can't fit through the opening." He eyed her up and down and made an hourglass motion with his hands. "You probably could." He took a few more steps toward her and tried to put his hands around her waist.

"Now just a minute, mister. Back off!" Melody scooted backward out of his reach.

"First of all, I just wanted to see if you would fit through the opening." His hands fell to his hips. "I'm not interested in you."

"I don't do small spaces," she said.

"You don't do small spaces, what's that supposed to mean?"

"I can't make it any clearer. I. Don't. Do. Small. Spaces. You know. I am claustrophobic." She took a deep breath. "And just what do you mean by 'not interested in you' comment? What's wrong with me?"

Zander shook his head. *Unbelievable.* "There's nothing wrong with you. I'm not interested in you or any other woman."

"Oh. I see." Melody's brows raised.

"What? Nuh-huh!" He rolled his eyes. "I need a breather. Why does the world judge you if you aren't in a relationship?"

She nodded. "I'm not judging. I'm not in a relationship, either."

"You aren't?"

"No," Melody answered.

Zander looked at her. The conversation suddenly had become awkward. How did they go from crawl spaces to relationship status in mere seconds? Sure, she was cute. Especially her pouting lips. But, after the way things had ended with Bria, he was not looking to be part of a couple. Zander couldn't even figure out how Melody had ended up at Sugar Plum Inn, but it didn't matter. The way it was snowing they were stuck with each other for a few days, if not more.

He was pretty sure he knew her type without even knowing her. She'd waltzed in here with her designer boots and clothes like she owned the place. She had even turned her nose up at the custom-made, bathtub. The princess only took showers, and now he found out she was claustrophobic, to boot. He'd had enough dealings with women like her to last him a lifetime.

"Look," he broke the shattering silence. "I really need your help with this."

"I can't!"

"Can't or won't?" he demanded.

"Why weren't those vents covered before now? It's the middle of February, for goodness sake!"

"We had a mild fall and winter ... until now, that is. I guess I just forgot they needed to be covered."

"Look, Zander. I would like to help you, I really would, but I can't. I just can't."

Zander had to find a way to convince her to help him. Those vents needed to be covered, and she was the only one small enough to fit through the crawl space. Normally he had a handyman take care of that detail, but he was gone for the winter. Zander had to conserve the heat as much as he could ... especially if the storm got worse and they lost power.

"Let's try this. How about coming upstairs with me? I will show you the crawl space, and you can decide then. What do you think? Can you manage to do that for me?"

"I guess." She put her finger up. "But just to look, Zander, that's all."

"I'll take it." He smiled. "Follow me."

Turning, he swiftly exited the kitchen and headed to the steps, with Melody following close behind. He took the steps two at a time and stopped in the middle of the hallway. He looked at Melody and pointed up. "It's just behind that trap door. I will slide it back for you. Then all you need to do is crawl through the opening."

"Zander." Melody tried to stop him from talking.

He continued, "then the eaves are in the front side of the house. Once you get through the space, there is enough room for you to crawl on your hands and knees."

"Zander, stop!" she yelled, watching him.

In one swoop he jumped up and pushed the sliding door aside. A cold puff of air blew down on them from the attic. "What?" he asked.

"How am I supposed to get up there?"

"I'll get you a chair. You can step on it. Look, it's not as bad as you think."

"Easy for you to say. You weren't the one trapped inside a steam trunk for hours."

"Oh," Zander mumbled. "Well, you've got me on that one. But seriously, Melody, it isn't that small." He rushed into the bathroom. He grabbed the chair, placing it under the opening. Next, he ran up the steps to his room and grabbed a flannel shirt and a pair of wool socks for her. "Here, put my shirt on over your sweater. It's cold up there, and it'll protect your sweater from snagging. I advise you to take off your boots and put a pair of my socks on. It might be a little tough moving around up there in heels." He handed Melody the socks and shirt.

"Zander!"

He watched as her face turned a shade of gray. "Let's take this one step at a time. Get the stuff on. I'll help you through the opening. You'll see it really isn't that bad." He patted the chair for her to step on.

Obeying, she timidly stepped up, shaking her head in protest. "I can't reach."

"Let me help you." And before she could protest, he was standing beside her on the chair, firmly planting his hands around her waist. "On the count of three. One ... two ..." Before he uttered three, he tightened his grip around her middle, hoisting her up into the opening.

"Zander!" Melody squealed, swinging her legs back and forth while holding on to the inside of the floor above. "Zander!"

Zander watched her legs thrashing back and forth. He noticed how slim they looked in the leggings. He wasn't quite sure of where he should place his hands now. The curvature of her hips looked inviting. Too inviting. But if not there, where? Cautiously, he placed his hands on her hips. They were firm beneath his touch. He lifted her high enough that she could crawl through the space, and his hands reluctantly released her.

CHAPTER 5

"ZANDER!" MELODY SCREAMED FROM THE touch of his hands on her hips. One minute she was standing on the chair, and the next she was hoisted into the crawl space.

She was on her hands and knees. The space was small and cold. The wind howled outside and blew in through the vents. She shivered, despite wearing both her sweater and his flannel shirt. Glancing in the direction of the eaves, she noticed that the snow was starting to come in. Slowly crawling on the wooden beams, she made her way toward the open vents.

He hollered up to her, "make sure you stay on the wooden beams. If not you'll fall through the floor."

"Anything else, Sergeant?" Melody grumbled sarcastically, loud enough for him to hear.

"Nope." Zander's tone was neutral. He chose to ignore the tone in her voice.

Great. Now she had to do a balancing act as well.

How in the world did she let this happen to her? Everything had happened so fast. One minute he was showing her the opening, and the next he was hoisting her through it. She could easily see that Zander wouldn't had fit through the opening. *Hurry up, Melody. Do what you've got to do and get out,* she thought, trying to give herself a pep talk. Doing a quick scan of the small space, she was glad it was bigger than the trunk she got stuck in years ago. It wasn't nearly as bad she had thought it would be. Still, she would never admit that to him. She had her pride to consider.

She took a deep breath and inched her way closer. She brushed the snow off the beams. Taking hold of the magnetic covering, she attached it to the first vent blocking the wind and snow from coming in. Crawling to the second eave, she did the same thing. After covering both vents she noticed a difference in the temperature. Not a lot, but enough. She made her way back to the small opening. Peering through, she saw Zander sitting on the chair, relaxing.

"How am I supposed to get down?"

Zander jumped up and stood on the chair. "That didn't take too long."

"It's cold up here, so if you don't mind?"

"Turn around and lie on your stomach. Slowly slide backward through the opening, and I'll guide your legs to the chair and help you down."

Melody did as he instructed, anticipating the touch of his hands again. Then she felt it. Zander's hands gripped her calves. His hands slid the whole way up each leg as she lowered, stabilizing them, until he was holding her waist again.

Letting her feet come to rest on the chair, she let out a huge sigh of relief. She realized they were standing a mere inch from one another, with his hands still around her waist. She liked how they felt around her middle. And tried to shake the feeling off.

He reached up and brushed a bit of snow from her hair. Stepping off the chair, he extended his hand, offering to help her step down. She took his hand and stepped down, standing next to him. Removing her hand, she began unbuttoning the flannel shirt he'd lent her. Their eyes locked. Neither of them said a word. She continued unbuttoning the flannel and slid it off her sweater.

Melody broke the trance and handed Zander his shirt. "Thanks. It was cold." Reaching down, she peeled the wool socks off and slid her boots back on.

Later that afternoon, with a mug of hot chocolate, Melody strolled from the kitchen into the living room. She claimed the window seat and tucked her legs beneath her. Closing her eyes, she took a long sip. Leaning back on the pillows, she reached for the blue afghan and pulled it over her legs.

She pulled the curtains back and gazed into the winter wonderland outside. It was still snowing. The gusty wind made the tree branches sway back and forth, and the snow whipped around, leaving nothing bare in its trail. Pennsylvania hasn't had this much snow at one time in years. It would figure Williamsport was on the cusp of a blizzard the few days she decided to get away. She gladly accepted the exchange, though. Hearts for snow. Glitter for solitude.

Letting the curtains fall back to their normal stance, she wrapped both hands around the warm mug. She closed her eyes as she savored the next sip. She smiled, remembering. It was a tradition of hers and Gabby's. Each time either of them came home from a date, they would stay up late talking. Sharing details while drinking hot chocolate.

Ping … Ping … Ping

Melody opened her eyes to the noise, casting her memory aside. "What was that?"

Ping … Ping

She tossed the afghan aside. Walking to the coffee table, she set her mug down and listened.

Ping … Ping … Ping … Ping

Melody walked toward the entryway and opened the door. A rush of cold air blew in, making her face scrunch. Then she saw it. Hail was bouncing off the porch steps.

Ping … Ping … Ping

She took a few steps onto the porch. Everything was becoming covered in a shiny white glaze. She folded her arms across her chest and came back inside. Closing the door, she saw Zander headed in her direction. He had his coat and boots on and carried a shovel.

"It's raining ice," she offered. Although she figured he already knew, since he was decked out in his winter gear.

"I know. I need to get the ice off the steps. The temps are dropping, and if the ice clings to the wood ... well, I'm sure you know how bad that could be."

"Be careful, Zander."

He paused for a second, offered a small smile, and went outside. He couldn't remember the last time someone said that to him. She watched from a window as he used the edge of his shovel to scrape, then push the ice off the top step. Satisfied, he stepped onto the next step and lost his footing.

Melody threw the door open. Zander was lying at the bottom of the steps in a snow drift. "Zander!" she ran outside and stopped at the edge of the porch. "Are you okay? I told you to be careful!" Slowly she made her way down each step until she reached him. Kneeling in the snow beside Zander, she looked at him and gently shook his shoulders. "Zander, Zander!"

"Please stop shaking me."

"You scared me half to death. Are you okay?"

"I'm still breathing." He sounded annoyed. He slowly sat up, covered with snow.

Melody reached toward Zander, brushing the snow off him, and started laughing. "I'm sorry, I don't mean to laugh. You should see yourself." She stood. Even though she had brushed snow off him, he was still covered in white. An outline of his body in the snow was all that remained of his mishap, and his cheeks were red from the cold air. Looping her arm through his, she helped him climb the steps to the porch.

"Thank you," he said with a flat tone. He stopped to brush more snow from his jeans. "You'd better get inside. You aren't wearing a coat." His tone was curt.

She let go of his arm. "Fine." She turned, perturbed from being dismissed. That's what she got for helping him earlier with the vents. He was the type of guy that only wanted help on his terms, when he needed something. He thanked her, but she could hear it in his voice, he really wasn't grateful that she helped him after he fell. She didn't need this. It was cold outside anyway. Extremely cold.

She marched toward the door. As she reached for the doorknob, a burst of cold, wet snow hit the back of her neck. Snow slid down the back of her sweater onto her skin. She stopped in her tracks, frozen. *He really didn't do that*, she thought as she turned to face Zander. He was standing a couple feet from her, armed with another round of white artillery. His eyes glistened mischievously, and his eyebrows waggled.

"Really?" Melody asked. Then it happened again, this time hitting the front of her sweater. A mist of snow ricocheted onto her face. "I can't believe you did that! Game on, mister!" She rushed to the porch banister and scooped a handful of snow and threw it in his direction, missing him. Taking another handful of white snow, she swiftly crossed to him. She released the snow in her hand, letting it cascade over the top of his head. The look of surprise washed across his face, as did the snow, and Melody started laughing. Before she knew what had happened, Zander grabbed her arm and pulled her closer to him. He was warm, he held her tight, and his brown eyes were friendly. She liked this new side of Zander. Melody felt him pull her in until they were nose to nose. She closed her eyes, hoping to feel his lips dance across hers. Where did that come from? She didn't know him. She had never wanted a stranger to kiss her before. Instead, she felt a gush of cold snow tumble onto her face. She opened her eyes to see Zander brushing the snow from his head and laughing.

"Take that," he said.

Her eyelashes caught the white flakes, causing her to blink a few times and Melody swatted his chest. "Not fair, you have a coat on."

"You're right, Melody," he conceded. "Let's get inside and get you warmed up." With that, Zander shuffled the both of them inside.

CHAPTER 6

"GREAT, STILL NO PHONE SIGNAL." Melody sighed as she plugged her phone in to charge it.

"And you probably won't get one ... at least while you're staying here," Zander injected his comments without being asked. "Especially in the middle of a snowstorm."

"So much for technology."

"I wouldn't know. Never use it. I prefer to stay off the grid." Zander grabbed an apple from the counter and took a bite.

"Seriously?" *It's the year 2020.* "Who does that?" Melody asked.

"Me, that's who." Zander mumbled between bites.

"No cell phone? No computer?" Melody crossed her arms in disbelief and leaned against the counter.

"Nope."

"No Twitter? No Instagram?" Her eyes squinted.

"Nada," Zander answered with a broad smile.

"No email?"

"Not a one!" he sounded proud. "I'll be back in about an hour. I have to check on the shed out back." Zander walked out before she had the chance to ask about some other type of gadgetry that she thought he ought to have. Stopping on the other side of the door, he opened it again, sticking his head inside. "And before you ask, none of that book stuff for the face either." He closed the door before she could argue.

"What?" she couldn't resist. Following Zander to the door, she opened it. "It's called Facebook!" she hollered in his direction, then closed the door, laughing.

She watched him cross the yard and enter the shed. The shed, as he called it. It was more like a small building. It was still snowing out. The snow reached mid-calf on Zander as he tromped through it. Every time the storm slowed, and she thought it would end, it picked up again, as either hail or snow. With no phone signal, there was no way to get ahold of Gabby and let her know she was okay.

Melody set the table for two. She crossed to the refrigerator and opened the doors. The freezer was completely empty, and there wasn't much left in the fridge, itself. Scanning the contents, she settled on bread and cheddar cheese along with a jar of applesauce. *This should be interesting.* Scouring the cupboards, she found baked beans to add to the menu.

She turned to her phone's play list before settling down to make grilled cheeses. Deciding on Herb Alpert, she played "This Guy's in Love with You" and begun humming along to the music. She smiled from the memory of her parents dancing to 'their song' when she was a little girl.

Zander walked into the kitchen and stopped in his tracks. He could hardly believe what he was seeing and hearing. Melody was humming to the music and partially dancing with the spatula as she went from the stove to the table. She fluttered across the floor to the music, and her lips moved, just a bit, while humming. Not sure how to make his presence known to her, Zander cleared his throat loud enough for her to hear. Melody whirled around in his direction.

"I didn't hear you come in," she stammered.

"Don't stop," Zander said while slipping his coat off, letting it crumple to the floor. In a few steps he was at her side. "May I have this dance?" He swallowed hard. Her lips were the shade of apricot, again.

"Um ... you mean ... with me?"

"Well, I certainly don't want to dance with the spatula." He liked the reaction he got from her. Melody was flustered, and it showed. Her cheeks flushed to a reddish tint. Maybe she wasn't like Bria. At first, she seemed just like his ex. But not now. Maybe it was time to move forward. Maybe. It was one dance. He wasn't marrying her, for goodness sake.

"Alright," she barely whispered loud enough for him to hear.

Zander slowly pulled her into his arms and began to lead them around the kitchen. She fit nicely in his arms. Their hands molded together while his other hand slid around to her back, gently guiding her to the music. His eyes locked with hers as he felt her breathing become heavier. The song came to an end, but he didn't care. He liked the way she felt in his arms. He would have continued dancing without the music. He didn't need music to dance. Just Melody. Slowly and regretfully, Zander broke his hold.

"Let's eat," he mumbled.

Melody tried to make small talk. The feel of Zander's arms wrapped around her was beginning to fade. She wished it wouldn't.

"Not a lot to choose from. Sandwiches, beans, and applesauce. Hope that's alright with you?"

"Are you kidding? A hot cheese sandwich on a cold winter's night. It's just the thing to warm up with." Zander took a large bite. "You're a Herb Alpert fan, huh?" He managed to say while chewing.

"My parents were." Melody took a small bite of her sandwich.

"Were?"

"Yes, they're both gone now." She smiled. "I used to watch them dance to "This Guy's in Love with You" at least once a week. My dad would surprise my mom when she least expected it by asking her to dance.

She never knew when. She would be washing dishes, doing laundry, or running the sweeper. It was his way of taking the mundane out of the mundane chores." She sighed and smiled. "Sometimes he would even ask Gabby or me to dance. And when we did, he twirled us around like little ballerinas."

Melody let her index finger draw imaginary circles on top of the table next to her plate. "I noticed this table last night. This is a beautiful piece of work. It belongs to the coffee table in the living room. Is it a set?"

"Wow ..." Zander raised one eyebrow. "Good eye. They're part of a set, along with the hutch behind you. I made them."

"Zander, you really made them?" Melody's mouth dropped open.

"Yes. It's maple, a strong wood that's moisture resistant, perfect for in the kitchen."

"I didn't know you're an artist."

"Well, I wouldn't exactly call myself an artist. I just like making things from wood."

"Wait a minute ... do you sell your work?" Melody asked.

"Here and there."

"Here and there!" She shook her head. "You need a website, Zander. You could seriously make a good living."

"Sorry. I fly off the grid, remember?" He stood, collected his dishes, and crossed to the sink.

Melody stood and brought her dishes to the sink too. "Look, Zander, I do marketing for a living. I know what I'm talking about. I could help you."

At that moment the lights flickered off and on.

"What was that?" she asked, looking around.

"It looks like we might lose power." Zander pulled the curtain back from the window that was above the sink and eyeballed the conditions outside. "It's snowing harder, and the wind is really whipping around." He turned to look at Melody just as the lights flickered off.

CHAPTER 7

AFTER WHAT SEEMED LIKE LONGER than a few minutes the lights flickered on again.

"Whew ... thank goodness," Melody mumbled. Realizing she was digging her fingers into Zander's hand, she quickly let go. She hadn't realized she'd taken hold of his hand when the lights went out. That was embarrassing. She didn't need comforting by a man. She was a strong woman ... perhaps too strong ... perhaps too independent.

She let her mind wander to Dillon. They'd dated for six months. She'd never really understood him. He worked hard for a living and was always on call. He worked for the Pittsburgh Police SWAT team. He didn't know how not to be an officer. He had no time for her romantic notions. He would have never danced with her in the kitchen as she made dinner. When he came home from work, that was it. He vegetated. In the end, Melody didn't blame him. Dillon had a stressful job. They were just two different people. They ended things on good terms.

"... and like I was saying," Zander continued, "you know it's really bad out when the moose are booking a room for the night."

"What's that?" Melody asked, trying to catch up with what he was saying and leaving her musings behind. "Wait ... moose!" She grabbed the hand towel that was lying on the counter and tossed it toward Zander.

Zander caught the towel. "Oh, you're listening to me, after all," he teased.

"I'm sorry," Melody laughed. "I guess I was somewhere else."

"A thousand miles away?"

"More like a couple months," she shared. "So, what happens if we lose power?"

"I have plenty of wood cut and ready to go in the fireplace. There should be extra blankets in the closet in your guest room and a flashlight or two in the nightstand."

"Great. I guess we just wait and see then."

"I'm headed to the shed for my emergency crank radio just in case the power goes out."

"I'll gather the extra blankets and flashlights."

"Sounds like a plan," Zander said, putting his coat on.

"Watch out for those moose," Melody hollered after him as he left.

Zander's thoughts continued gravitating back to Melody. He thought he knew her type. He had her pegged as another Bria. Someone that always had to have things her way. Melody showed up at Sugar Plum Inn wearing her designer boots and clothes, demanding that she had made a reservation.

She'd made a fuss of the fact there was only a tub and no shower, not to mention the lack of heat in the bathroom. He didn't see what the big deal was. No heat kept a person moving in the morning. Of course, when he'd started the impromptu snowball fight Melody had joined right in, laughing the whole time. Bria never would have. And when he asked Melody to dance while she was cooking dinner, she wholeheartedly accepted. Bria never would have done that. She would have grumbled the whole time.

It was crazy for Zander to keep comparing Melody to Bria. To even think about Melody unhinged him. It was preposterous. Foolish. Absurd. She was a guest. A stranger. She walked into his life and would be walking back out of it on Sunday. Of course, with the way the snow was coming down, she would probably be here a little longer.

Zander didn't understand it himself. Why the comparison between Melody and Bria? It wasn't as if a relationship could be formed amongst themselves. He was just fine with his status quo. These thoughts were just gathering cobwebs because he'd found out that Melody was not in a relationship either.

Melody awakened to a deep chill in the air and the sound of Zander knocking on her door. Melody sat up, pulling the blankets with her. "Come in," she hollered while shivering.

Zander wasted no time entering. His eyes darted to her sitting up in bed with the quilt pulled up to her chin. "We lost power sometime during the night," he offered what was already obvious.

"It sure seems that way." Melody reached up running her fingers through her hair.

For a few minutes Zander seemed frozen in place, watching her play with her hair. Realizing he was holding onto his gray cable knit sweater, he cleared his throat forcing him to stay focused. "Here." He took a few steps closer to the bed and laid his sweater on the edge. "You'll need this. I'm going to start a fire downstairs. This house can get cold quickly with no heat, so I suggest we stay in the living room for the heat."

"Sure. How long do you think it'll be out?"

"I have no idea. Not for long, I hope." He turned and walked toward the door, pausing with his back toward her. "Good news, though, you get to take a bath with no heat." He laughed, opening the door, and slipped into the hallway before she could react to his comment.

"Zander!" she hollered and threw one of the pillows at the door. "You're so not funny!"

Melody was thankful for the sweater Zander let her wear. Standing in front of the fire that roared in the fireplace, she warmed her hands. She didn't notice Zander had joined her in the living room.

"Nice, isn't it?" he asked, sitting on one of the couches.

"Oh, Zander, I didn't see you come in." She sat across from him on the other couch. "It is. I don't remember the last time I stood around a fire. It's very relaxing."

"I'm glad you think so."

Melody smiled. "You probably make a lot of fires living here."

"Every now and again. Warm enough?"

"Yes, thank you." Melody wrapped the oversized sweater tighter across her front. "It's comfortable. You may find yourself without a sweater when I leave."

"Hmm," he raised his eyebrows. "My ex wouldn't be caught dead wearing her boyfriend's sweater. Fashion faux pas for her." His cheeks reddened a little and he coughed. "Hungry? There are a couple of biscuits left in the basket on the counter."

"That sounds good." Melody stood, eager to drop the subject. "I think I'll do that. Are you coming?"

"No, I ate already. I'm going to grab some more wood for the fire."

As Melody sauntered into the kitchen, she slid her hands into the sweater pockets. She felt something inside one of them. Pulling the object from the pocket she gasped. In her hand sat a small, red velvet box. Looking over her shoulder to make sure she was by herself she pried the box open. *Oh my*. Inside the box sat a white-gold engagement ring. The center diamond was a princess cut and sparkled unlike anything she had ever seen before. The center stone was surrounded by smaller diamonds. Gently she let her finger trace over the ring. It was gorgeous.

Swiftly she snapped the lid closed and deposited it back into the pocket. Obviously, it belonged to Zander. Melody's mind swirled like the wind outside. Zander must have forgotten that he put the ring in his sweater. He was about to become engaged. However, he'd told her he wasn't in a relationship. Why would he do that? He didn't need to lie. After all, she was just a stranger staying in his inn. She would be leaving tomorrow, if the weather cooperated, and they would never see each other again. Was the girl in the turned-down picture on the fireplace mantel the recipient? That would certainly explain why he'd laid it down. He didn't want Melody to see his bride-to-be.

Melody decided upon an apple instead of a biscuit. Taking it, she headed back into the living room. The fire emitted a welcoming warmth. Her eyes lingered on the picture frame on top of the mantel. It was too tempting. She wanted to stand the picture back up. Should she? She decided against it.

In the end, she reasoned, it really shouldn't matter to her ... but for some reason it did matter. And she needed to figure out why. She felt a strange, uncomfortable longing to find that Zander was honest. She needed to figure out why. At the same time, she felt a small twinge of sadness for the woman in the picture. Did she really know Zander? Did the woman really know what she was getting herself into? What would she think about Zander turning her picture down? How would she feel to hear Zander say he wasn't in a relationship?

Melody tossed the apple core into the fire and sat down on the couch, pulling the afghan over her legs to ward off the chill.

CHAPTER 8

"MELODY," ZANDER GREETED HER AS he walked into the living room with a red box in his hand. "Look what I found." He set the box on the middle of the coffee table.

"What's that?" Melody mumbled, not really interested. She couldn't take her mind off the ring she found.

"Scrabble. Ever played?"

"Once or twice." She looked at him as he sat across from her on the other couch.

"Well, well, well! That's perfect." He clapped his hands, rubbing them together. "This is just what we need to pass the time while we wait for the power to come back on." He flashed her a quick smile. "What do you say?" Zander began setting up the game board, not bothering to wait for Melody's answer.

Slowly she slid her legs from their haven under the afghan and sat on the edge of the couch. "I guess. You go first."

"It'll be my pleasure, Ms. Chambers, my pleasure indeed," he replied. "Let's see," he said, looking at his letters aligned in front of him. "R–i–n–g." He looked at her and wrote his points down. "Only five points. Your turn." He motioned toward the board.

Melody stared at the word. Why did he choose that word? Was he trying to tell her something? Melody let out a long sigh and shuffled the little wooden tiles to build a word. "Let's see, b–r–a–g." She smiled. "I believe that's 14 points."

"G–r–o–o–m. Seven points for me." Zander eagerly added his points.

"That gives you a total of 12. You do realize my first word was 14?"

Zander retorted. "Build your word." His eyes squinted. "Unless you can't."

Melody placed her letters on the board. "That's 7 points for g-a-m-e." She eyed Zander while she picked her new tiles. Sooner or later, she wanted to ask him about the ring. "Your turn."

"I know, I know," he answered, a little unnerved. "B-r-i-d-e, which gives me 16 points and a grand total of 18." He looked smugly at her.

He's taking this game too seriously. "Okay, hotshot, take this, d–i–c–e–r. That gives me 11 points, which brings me to a total of 32." It was her turn to look smug.

Zander pushed his sleeves up and cracked his knuckles. "I've got this."

Melody giggled. *He's got this.* She rolled her eyes. He was competitive.

He slowly chanted the letters to his next word. "D–r–e–s–s–e–d." Zander pointed at Melody and grinned. "That is a word score of 22, bringing my total to 50. Did you hear that Melody, 50!" He stood up and patted himself on the back. "And," while sitting back down he added, "by the way, I saw you roll your eyes. Scared?"

"Of you?" she chuckled. "Ha!" she added two letters to the board, spelling o-r-t.

"What *is* that?" he asked. "That's not a word."

"It most certainly is to. That gives me 5 points, with an overall total of 38. Write it down."

"What's the definition?"

"You are incorrigible, aren't you?" She stared at him. What was his problem? "It means a scrap of food left over from a meal." She pointed toward the paper Zander was using to keep score. "Go ahead." She stood and started to walk around the table.

She couldn't believe he wasn't writing her measly 5 points down. Zander ignored her. She eyed him as he continued to spell his next word. Was he really disregarding the roles of the game?

"S-p-r-i-n-g," he proudly announced and leaned back against the couch, adding his total to the score. "Word score of 10, making my total 60."

"You owe me points," Melody demanded.

"Sorry, that's not a word, and we don't have a dictionary to prove otherwise." Zander smiled, folding his arms across his chest.

This guy is not only competitive, he is egotistic. Melody reached down to snatch the pencil and pad, but he slid it just out of her reach. "You can't do that! You're a sore loser! And what's worse, you're a sore winner," Melody scolded. Reaching further, she leaned across his legs, trying to snatch the pad. Then she heard it, the thud on the floor.

Melody froze for an instant, afraid to move. She knew what that noise was. It was the ring. It had fallen out her pocket. She slowly straightened. Zander's face had gone ashen, and he stared at the red velvet box lying on the floor.

CHAPTER 9

ZANDER REACHED DOWN WITH ONE scoop of his hand, snatching the box off the floor. Had he really forgotten to take it out of that sweater? His eyes met Melody's. The look across her face told him she knew exactly what was in the box. A memory he had tried to forget. Without realizing it, his mulling's carried him back to that evening.

It was Thanksgiving. His favorite holiday. He and Bria, along with a small group of friends, had spent the afternoon enjoying all the trimmings of a delicious meal. Bria had prepared turkey, stuffing, mashed potatoes, gravy, veggies, bread, and a variety of pies for dessert. She had even made him his favorite pie, raisin. He remembered how much she had grumbled about being stuck in the kitchen working while he relaxed in the other room. Why hadn't he noticed that then?

Everyone had left for the evening. It was lightly snowing, and a cool November chill began to set in.

Zander started a fire and threw several pillows and quilts on the floor, trying to set the mood for a relaxing evening. Just the two of them, a fire, and two glasses of red wine.

After getting comfortable in the small oasis Zander had prepared for them, he reached into his sweater pocket. Pulling the velvet box out and opening it, he saw a look on Bria's face that no one should see seconds before proposing. He forged ahead anyway.

"Bria, I love you and want to marry you. Will you marry me?"

"Um ... Zander, I'll have to think about it." She flatly stated with a blank stare.

"Oh." He snapped the box closed and cleared his throat, trying to recover from his proposal gone wrong. "What's there to think about?"

"It's been a long day. We have a lot to talk about, and it's getting late."

"Like what? I love you. You love me." He could feel his mood changing, and not for the better. Zander was frustrated. He had rehearsed this evening. It was not going according to plan.

"Zander, do we really have to do this now?"

"Yes, Bria, we do."

She sighed and shifted away from him. "Fine. You're happy living in this made-up world of yours, tucked away in the woods of Williamsport. I'm not. I want more out of life." Bria forced a smile.

Zander felt tension lodge in his neck and shoulders. A small headache was forming at his temples. Was he hearing her correctly? His head was spinning. Everything seemed to be moving in slow motion. Zander could see Bria standing up and slipping her coat on. He saw her lips moving, but the ringing in his ears prevented him from hearing anything she was saying. He didn't see this coming. She said she loved him. Standing up, he heard the last few things she was trying to convey.

"Aunt Tulu gave me this place so she could travel. But I don't want to run it either. I've been offered a great job in New York, and I've decided to take it."

"What? You're leaving?" Zander sputtered. "When?"

"Tomorrow."

"What about this place? Who's going to run it?"

"I don't know. I don't have all the details worked out yet. Look, you can stay in the small room in the shed, at least temporarily, until I figure out what to do with the inn."

"Bria, you can't be serious."

Bria leaned closer and kissed him on the cheek. "Goodbye, Zander." Then she walked out the door.

"Zander. Are you listening?" Melody asked, cutting through his thoughts.

"What?" he shook his head and shoved the box into his jeans. "What were you saying?"

"You don't have to hide the ring. I already saw it." Melody pushed the game aside and sat on the edge of the coffee table facing him. She folded her hands together, resting them on her lap. "I saw it while I was in the kitchen."

"Oh."

"Why did you lie to me?" Melody kept her tone plain, yet stern.

"I didn't lie to you."

"You told me you weren't in a relationship, but it clearly seems that you are. You're about to become engaged. I'm going to assume it is to the woman in the picture on the mantel." One of her eyebrows raised in question.

"I'm not. And yes. She was the one. I forgot I put the ring in my sweater. I haven't worn that sweater since Thanksgiving."

Melody seemed to consider that. Then she nodded slowly. "Oh." She crossed to the fireplace.

Zander went to Melody and put his hands on her shoulders, turning her to look at him. "I want to explain. Her name is Bria. I asked her to marry me Thanksgiving evening. She said no." He removed the box from his pocket and placed it on top of the mantel.

"Oh my," Melody whispered. "That explains why you took her picture down."

"We were together for five years. I was convinced she was the one. I guess she didn't think so. She accepted a job in New York and left. She didn't want a furniture designer who lives in the middle of nowhere. She was much too refined." He scrubbed his face with his hands. It still hurt.

"But your work is beautiful." Melody ducked under his hold and started picking up the game that was scattered across the coffee table. "I'd be proud to be engaged to someone that made such beautiful creations." He saw her cheeks redden. She kept her eyes downward, focusing on gathering the little wooden tiles.

The silence between them was suddenly awkward.

Zander rubbed the back of his neck with one hand and slid the other into the front pocket of his blue jeans. "It's getting dark. I'm going to bring more logs in for the fire and light some candles."

"Good idea." Melody sighed. "How about I see what I can put together for dinner?"

"Sure. There is a jar of matches next to the stove. Are you able to light the pilot light?"

"I think so. But only if I need to. I won't open the refrigerator. I will see what I can find in the cupboards to heat up." She turned to go into the kitchen.

Zander removed the picture of Bria from the mantle and tossed it into the fire. When he heard Melody gasp, he forced a smile for her benefit. "I should have done that a while ago."

"I'm sorry." She spoke with such tenderness.

Had he ever felt such sympathy from Bria? His heart warmed. "Don't be." He was suddenly self-conscious. "Sometimes a person needs to find another bridge to end up where they're supposed to be." Not wanting to hear her reply, he shrugged his shoulders and left.

CHAPTER 10

About an hour later Zander reappeared in the kitchen just as Melody put the final touches on their dinner. He wasn't even sure what they were having, but she wasn't grumbling to herself about having to pull together a dinner in these conditions. Instead of mumbling, she was humming a light tune. He couldn't decipher what she was humming but he could tell that she was content and happy to be preparing dinner. He wasn't used to that. In fact, it was refreshing after listening to Bria complain about cooking all the time.

Zander took a deep breath and decided not to compare Melody to Bria again. There wasn't a whole lot he knew about Melody, but the one thing he did know was, she was a special woman. She had been great company the last couple of days. She didn't mind the simple things, where showers weren't concerned. And he longed to know her better. Melody had lit the candles that sat in the middle of the table and set two place settings close to one another.

Zander purposely shuffled his boots across the floor for Melody to hear. He didn't want to startle her in the darkened room.

She whipped her head around at the sound and smiled. She looked lovely in the candlelight. As he got closer Zander could still see the outline of her apricot lips. He still found them desirable. He would had preferred to stand there admiring her all evening, but the growling inside his stomach demanded otherwise.

"What's on the menu for tonight?"

"Step into my office, Zander, and see for yourself." Melody waved her hand toward the table. "Tonight we'll dine on the best pancakes in the state of Pennsylvania and quench our thirst with delectable hot chocolate." She giggled. "Please have a seat and help yourself to this fine fare."

"Thank you, my lady!" Zander did as she directed. They each had a stack of pancakes piled high on their plates with a mug of hot chocolate. How could this woman possibly know pancakes were his favorite food? Somehow, Melody managed to turn the simple meal into the most delightful looking cuisine that would give any five-star restaurant a run for their money.

"Well," she said sitting next to him. "What do you think?" she held her breath while drizzling syrup over her pancakes. She had hoped he didn't mind the simple meal.

"Candlelight and pancakes," he said, and purposely gazed into her cedar eyes that captured the dancing flames of the candles. "Perfect, absolutely perfect." He reached for her hand gently, taking it in his and caressing it with his thumb. "Pancakes are my favorite. Happy Valentine's Day." He released her hand. "Let's eat."

Melody's heart swelled in her throat. *Was he serious?* Pancakes were really his favorite food? And Valentine's Day. How could she possible forget what today was? This was her favorite holiday. She blinked hard several times, forcing the emerging tears back where they belonged and hoping he didn't notice in the darkness. She had completely blocked February14th from her mind. The first time in her thirty-two years. But then again, isn't that why she'd left Pittsburgh? She'd succeeded. She'd managed to escape all the hearts and glitter and completely forgotten about the most romantic day of year.

"Happy Valentine's Day to you to, Zander."

The two of them made small talk between bites. Giggling over the similarities they shared. Such as: they both loved to drink hot chocolate. His favorite meal was pancakes and hers an old-fashioned fried egg sandwich served on toast. They also enjoyed taking long walks outside. The weather didn't matter. They each savored the fresh air and the stillness it offered for times of meditation and reflection.

"I'm stuffed!" Melody exclaimed, pushing her plate aside. "You know something?"

"What's that?" he mumbled through his last bite.

"I completely forgot about it being Valentine's Day. This used to be my favorite holiday." She picked up her mug and took a sip. "People always tell me that I have an old soul. I guess I am just a romantic softy."

"You said, used to be ... what happened, if you don't mind me asking?" Zander leaned back in his chair folding his arms.

"Dillon, for one. He has such a stressful job working for SWAT. It completely drained him. Leaving nothing for us. We ended our relationship on good terms six months ago and went our separate ways."

"I kind of sense there's something else."

"Sort of." Melody leaned back in her chair, taking small sips of her hot chocolate. "I don't want to bore you with my stories."

"I told you mine, and besides, it's not like we don't have the time."

"Fair enough." She set her empty mug back on the table next to her plate. "My parents were romantics. They were always doing little things for each other. I told you about the dancing while my mother did housework." Zander nodded as she continued. "They always hugged and kissed, whether they were leaving or coming."

"What else?" Zander was curious.

"My mother chilled easily and hated stepping out of a hot shower. Every day my father would grab her bath towel and throw it in the dryer while she showered. Just for a minute or two to warm it for her. And my mother knew how much he enjoyed homemade cookies. So, every day while he went to work, she made a different batch of cookies. He would enjoy a few cookies each evening after dinner."

"They worked hard on preserving their relationship."

"They did. But for them, it wasn't work. It was the simple pleasure of being in love with their best friend and making each other's lives enjoyable." Melody sighed. "So, I guess whoever I dated, I held to the same standards. Which was a pretty hard act to follow."

"I like that they did that for each other."

"Me too."

The lights flickered on and off a few times before finally staying on. A deep heaviness settled within Melody. She was actually enjoying not having power and dining by candlelight. She also knew that tomorrow was the day she had to leave Sugar Plum Inn and go back home. Something she wasn't altogether sure she was ready to do. What was wrong with her? Did she really believe in fate? Or was it a matter of simple convenience? It was an illusion. A simple matter of her wanting what her parents had.

Slowly she stood and blew the candles out, one at a time.

Melody awoke the next morning to an exceptional quiet and peacefulness in the air. She stayed in bed a little longer than usual, procrastinating for the first time in her life. She felt like a child again, having to go back to school after the end of summer vacation. Her stomach stirred with nervousness. Why wasn't she excited to be going back home to her life? Her sister and friends were back in Pittsburgh, not to mention Holly, her cat. The poor thing probably thought she was abandoned. Melody also had her job to go back to. Her supposedly dream job working for a greeting card company.

Then there was Zander. He was different. Each day he'd managed to capture a tiny bit more of her heart. How had he done it? It was just the two of them riding a snowstorm out. This wasn't real life. They were living a fantasy.

Sighing, she threw the blankets off and sank her toes into the rich rug. Warmth encircled her toes, and she wiggled them a bit, enjoying the heat, along with the power. Standing at the window, she pulled the curtains back. She could see Zander digging her RAV4 out of the snow. He made it look effortless.

Melody caught up with Zander in the kitchen. She had started to pack but decided to finish later that morning. He had just finished making a mug of cocoa for her. As she took the mug from him, their fingers lingered against each other for a moment. Each aware of which day it was and neither quite ready to accept it. Or willing to admit it to the other.

Melody took a deep breath. "I saw you cleaning the snow from my car. Thank you."

"No worries. I was up early. What time are you taking off?" He didn't move his fingers.

"I'm not sure yet. There's a good bit of white stuff out there." She set the mug on the counter. She had only managed to take a few sips of the velvety goodness. She didn't have much of an appetite this morning.

What had come over her? She never acted this way before. "Maybe I should ..." her voice trailed off. It was too much to hope for. For her to possibly think that he would ask her to stay another night, was too much. Their eyes met and locked.

"Maybe you should." Zander stated.

Did she hear him correctly? Did he really agree? "Maybe I will," she whispered, willing him to say it.

"Yeah?" Zander asked.

"You know, just in case," she added. Afraid to look away. She felt like they were back in middle school. The two of them were talking in code, trying to say the same thing without really saying it. They were tiptoeing in the awkward conversation of adolescence instead of two mature adults saying what they were really feeling.

"I agree ... just in case."

"Good," Melody mumbled.

"Good." Zander grabbed his coat. "Now that's settled, can I show you something?"

"Sure. What's up?"

"It's a surprise."

"A surprise, for me?" her heart fluttered with anticipation. What kind of surprise? If he only knew how much Melody loved surprises.

"Get your coat and come with me."

Stepping outside the crisp morning air took her breath away. She hadn't been outside for what felt like days. She missed the feeling of rejuvenation of being outdoors. She glanced around. It had stopped snowing, and the sun shone brilliantly, making the snow sparkle. It was as if she was transformed into a winter wonderland.

The morning sun peeked through the snow lined trees. Neither said a word as Zander led her toward the shed. The freshly fallen snow was barren of human footprints. There were only a few traces of rabbit and deer prints. The two of them continued walking around the shed. Melody wondered what Zander wanted to show her.

As they rounded the back of the shed, she saw the massive weeping willow. The majestic branches were lined with snow, stretching far and curved downward. It was beautiful.

Zander turned, taking Melody's hand in his. "We're almost there." He continued holding her hand as they walked closer to the tree. Standing directly in front of it, he parted a few of the snow-covered branches that hung like a stage curtain, and they slipped between them.

Melody's eyes widen. Letting go of Zander's hand, she took a few more steps. She felt like she had just entered a fairytale. A once-upon-a-time land that all little girls dream of.

Glass candle holders hung from the bending branches. Battery-operated candles glowed inside of them, and the flames flickered against the snow. Melody slowly turned in a complete circle, arms flung out from her sides, laughing in delight.

"Oh, Zander ..." she exclaimed. "It's beautiful in here. Absolutely beautiful!" She stopped spinning and gazed into his eyes. "You did this?"

He nodded, smiling.

"But there were no footprints in the snow on the way up here. How?"

"I brushed over them on my way back to the inn." Zander winked.

"It's stunning," she chimed, spinning in another circle once more. "Zander, oh Zander, this is the nicest surprise I've ever gotten."

"Yeah?"

"Yeah ..." Melody barely whispered loud enough for him to hear.

Zander took a few steps closer, gently pulling her in his arms. She gazed up at him. He understood her. He had known how to speak to that romantic part of her soul. She felt as if the two of them, standing under the branches of the weeping willow, were the only ones who mattered in the world. He was Adam and she was Eve. No one else existed. It was perfect. He was all she needed.

Melody knew at that very second, inside the magical portrait he'd painted for her, she was in love.

"This is where I come to think." Zander shared. "I've never showed this to anyone before."

"I love it!" She closed her eyes and opened them again. "You make my heart smile!"

Zander leaned closer, resting his forehead against Melody's. Her lips beckoned to him. He answered, letting his lips float across hers. "Let's head back to the house."

Hand in hand, they did just that.

Just as they were about to go inside, Melody stopped. "Wait, Zander, have you ever made a snow angel?"

"Never."

"Let's do it!" A wide smile appeared across her face. "Right here."

"Now?"

"Yes, now!"

"Why not," Zander agreed.

The two of them lay on the fresh snow, moving their arms and legs back and forth. They were so caught up in making the angels and laughing they never heard the back door of the house open and close.

Melody saw the designer boots standing at Zander's head a moment after he did. Immediately he sat up. "Bria, what are you doing here?"

CHAPTER 11

"WHAT ARE *YOU* DOING AND who is *that?*" the woman named Bria motioned toward Melody, who had sat up as well. "I'll be in the kitchen when you're through playing games." She turned on her heels and went inside without saying another word.

Zander stood up, stretching his hands toward Melody to help her get up. "I have no idea what she is doing here, Melody," he offered.

Melody smiled and brushed the snow off her jeans. "No need to explain things to me." She forced herself to look at Zander. She didn't want to. The fairytale had melted. Too good to be true. "I need to finish packing, and you, it seems, have business to tend to." She scurried inside disappointed before he could answer her. She always had the worse timing. Leave it to her to fall in love with a guy right before his ex-fiancée showed up.

What was she thinking? How could she allow herself to fall in love with him? She didn't know him. She was a guest staying in the inn. This wasn't real life. It was something that only happens in movies. Today she was going back home. Anyway, it wasn't like Zander had any feelings toward her. At least he never spoke of them, if he did.

Closing the door to her guest room, she leaned her back against it. But then there was the tree. Why would he make such a grand romantic gesture toward her? It didn't matter now. It was time to shake those thoughts loose and finish packing. Her life was in Pittsburgh, not Williamsport.

Zander went into the kitchen, shedding his coat. He tossed it onto the counter.

Bria was sitting by the table. Her legs were crossed, and she glared at him.

"Bria," he started cautiously. "You're back in town." Bria's hair was shorter than before, but her scowl was familiar.

"Nice to see you too, Zander," she retorted. "By what I just saw outside, you've decided our five years together meant nothing."

"I didn't walk out on those five years, Bria," he said, calmly. He sat on the chair next to her. "Why aren't you in New York?"

"I've changed my mind," she stated.

Zander let out a big sigh. "What does that even mean? About what?"

"You and me, silly."

"What!" He stood up and began pacing. How could she do this? A couple of months ago she wanted nothing to do with him. With them. And now she did? "What about your job? What about you wanting more out of life?"

"Like I said, I change my mind."

Zander stopped and looked at Bria and began pacing again. She can't do that. Can she? He couldn't do this. He had moved on. And there was Melody ... was it fate? Zander wasn't even sure if he believed in fate. But there was Melody. His thoughts drifted back to the first time he saw her. She was so sure she'd made a reservation, even though the inn wasn't open. "I'm here," she'd proudly announced to him.

"Zander, are you listening to me?" Bria blurted, interrupting his thoughts. "Did you hear anything that I just said?"

Zander looked at her. Her left hand was stretched in his direction, and her fingers pranced up and down. She was actually waiting for him to slide the engagement ring onto her finger. "I'm listening, Bria." He stopped pacing and looked into her eyes. "I don't understand, but I'm listening." The pacing began again.

Bria stood and walked toward Zander, stopping him. "Listen, Zander, I made a mistake. I should have never gone to New York. We belong together. Here." She waved her hand, motioning to the inn. "Running this place. Together."

"What's with the change of heart?" He walked around her and began pacing again. "A couple months ago you complained about making Thanksgiving dinner. You wanted more out of life, you said."

"Look, you're right. I don't like slaving in a kitchen all day. That's not me. We can just go out on holidays, and problem solved."

Zander looked at Bria. "And what about my furniture designs?"

"Oh, Zander, don't be ridiculous. You could never make a living from your furniture creations. A hobby is one thing, but *that's not* a career. I mean seriously, what would I even tell my friends you did for a living?" She took a few steps closer to Zander, who was now leaning up against the counter. "Now, if you stop this nonsense and just put the ring on my finger, we can pretend none of this ever happened." She held up her left hand and smiled.

Zander stared at Bria while grabbing his coat and walked outside without saying another word.

Melody pulled the zipper shut on her suitcase and sat next to it on the edge of the bed. It was time to leave. Time to go back to her life. Her real life.

A knock sounded on her door.

Melody's heart leapt. It was Zander, it had to be. She rushed to the door, throwing it open. "Zander …"

"No, not Zander. Bria." The woman stated and strolled passed Melody into the room. She stopped, turning to face her with a smug look. "How long has this been going on with you and Zander?"

"Brie," Melody answered, hoping her voice didn't betray her outrage. "I don't understand."

"Bria, dear, Bria." The woman pursed her lips and folded her arms.

"Bria," Melody corrected. "If you're referring to Zander, nothing has been going on. I've only known him for three days."

"Three days. Oh my." Bria burst out laughing, bringing her left hand up toward her neck, playing with her chain. She was twisting and turning her wrist until she was sure Melody saw the engagement ring on her finger. "Well, I've known Zander for five years." She held her left hand up, displaying all five fingers, along with the diamond, for good measure.

"I know. He told me." Melody's eyes gazed at the ring. It was the same ring she had found in the sweater pocket. The engagement ring Zander had bought for Bria and the very ring Bria had turned down. Or had she? Why was she wearing it now? That didn't take long.

Zander had lied. He'd said it was over with Bria. He'd even thrown her picture in the fireplace, telling Melody it was time for him to move on. And the second Bria was back, he'd proposed to her again. "Look." She swallowed hard at the hot lump growing in her throat. She would not show this woman that she was affected by her and Zander's engagement. "I made reservations for the weekend. I was checking out today. There is nothing going on between Zander and myself."

"But *my* inn isn't even open for business."

"Wait. Your inn. Sugar Plum Inn belongs to you?" Melody found herself growing flustered and confused.

"Of course, silly. Who did you think it belonged to? Oh, you ..." Bria pointed to Melody. "You thought it belonged to my fiancée! Is that what he told you?" Bria laughed. "Oh my, no!"

Melody's ears started ringing. She thought she was going to be sick. Her stomach churned. Another lie? Zander was a player. He led her to believe that he was the owner. He threw her picture in the fire. Instinctively, Melody grabbed her stomach as it rattled. This was nothing but a big joke at her expense! *How stupid! How utterly stupid to fall for his shenanigans,* she chided herself.

She looked at Bria. She was standing next to the bed with a look of satisfaction imbedded on her face. There was even a small smile quivering, begging to be released instead of being held captive. Melody snatched her suitcase and coat off the bed and quickly retreated down the stairs and out to her car. Opening the front passenger side door, she tossed her things on the front seat and closed the door. Then she crossed to the driver's side. Pausing for a moment, she glanced up toward the window of what had been her room. Bria was standing there watching her.

Climbing in and shutting the car door, Melody started the ignition. She shifted into gear and pulled away. She was going back home where she belonged. Against her better judgement, she stole one last glance at the window where Bria was standing and saw Zander standing next to her. She drove around the bend in the road, and the image of them disappeared.

CHAPTER 12

It was a long drive back home. Melody was glad it wasn't snowing. The roads were void of any traces of snow left after the storm. She was relieved to be going back home. She let her mind wander on the drive. How could she possibly let herself begin to have feelings for Zander? That wasn't like her. She'd just met him.

Where was this craziness coming from? Surely it wasn't just because she loved Valentine's Day and had romanticized the whole idea. If that was the case, she had been doing that her whole life. No wonder as an adult she always seemed to be let down on February 14. She filled that day high with expectations. So much so, that the men she dated couldn't live up to her ideals. Any of them.

Was she wrong to want romance in her life? To be wooed? Was this just a silly school-girl's idea of what love was supposed to be? Or perhaps was it an effect of watching too many romantic movies? Working for a greeting card company certainly didn't help much. Was everyone right about her having an old soul? Maybe she was just longing for an era gone by. Now everything was taken over by technology and impersonal gestures.

But then again, was it wrong to expect honesty from people? It wasn't fair to be lied to and led on by someone. Everyone deserved to be respected. Maybe, just maybe, it was time for her to put away her school-girl ideas and face the reality that times had changed. People in today's world just didn't seem to have the time or care about those things anymore. She just had to accept the fact that she was born in the wrong century.

A few days had passed since Melody arrived home, and little by little she had gathered all the items she had saved over the years. She set a box on her kitchen table, tossing in her vintage Hollie Hobby dolls. She added the vintage Valentine's Day cards she had collected since she was in high school.

Satisfied, she bent down, picking up her cat. Cradling her in her arms and petting her, Melody spoke. "No more silliness and school-girl notions, Holly. Looks like it's me and you for the long haul. What do you think about that girl?"

Just then there was a knock on her door. The cat jumped from her arms and ran into another room. "Chicken!" Melody yelled after her as she went to answer the door.

She threw open the door to find Gabby standing with two thermoses in her hands. "Gabby!" Melody was surprised. "What are you doing here?'

Gabby thrust her hands forward. "Just like old times, remember? Can I come in? It's freezing out here!"

"Yes, yes, of course." Melody stepped aside, letting her sister enter.

Gabby marched straight into the living room, setting the thermoses on the coffee table and shedding her coat. Smiling, she looked at Melody. "We're recreating our date-night ritual. Remember?"

"I remember." Melody sat on the couch. "Except this isn't date night." She looked at her older sister. Gabby's stomach was no longer flat. It protruded, announcing that she was pregnant. She had long brown hair like Melody, but her eyes were a shade of sky-blue instead of the cedar color of Melody's.

"No, but I want to hear what happened with you at that inn." Gabby opened the thermoses filled with hot chocolate and handed one to her sister. "Spill it, sis! Ever since you've been back you haven't been yourself."

"Seriously?"

"Seriously!"

"Fine." Melody took a sip of the hot liquid and sighed. "Zander is the owner of Sugar Plum Inn, or so I thought ..."

"Go on," her sister encouraged, pulling her legs up onto the couch and stretching them across, coming to rest on Melody's lap.

"Well, at first he was kind of standoffish. You know, not happy that I was there. Insisting that I didn't have a reservation, but I did. Then a little at a time, he started to come around. Turns out that Zander has a fun and even romantic side to him, and ..."

"And?"

"And, I don't know. I started having feelings toward him. Or at least I thought I did. But it really doesn't matter in the end because of Bria."

"Wait, who's Bria?"

"His fiancée."

"His what?" Gabby blurted and set her hot chocolate back onto the coffee table.

"Well, first she was his ex-fiancée and then his fiancée again. Not to mention the real owner of Sugar Plum Inn. Not Zander." Melody sighed. "But there was this tree in the snow, and it was lit with candles, and we made snow angels and ..."

"I have to admit, Melody, I am thoroughly confused right this second."

"Me too, Gab, me too."

"But I have never seen you like this before."

"Like what?" Melody scrunched her nose.

"In love, little sister."

Melody jumped off the couch and started pacing back and forth. "No way! Nope! That's preposterous!"

"Is it?"

"He's a complete stranger and only has a bathtub, I might add."

Her sister laughed. "You're the one who said he was fun and romantic."

Melody stopped pacing and looked at Gabby. "And he designs the most beautiful pieces of furniture." She returned to pacing.

"Go on ..." Gabby said, her eyes sparkling with amusement.

"This is ridiculous." Melody stopped pacing again and looked at her sister. Gabby seemed to be enjoying this little persiflage a bit too much. "And an excellent dancer." She began pacing again.

"My work here is done." Gabby stood.

"But what did I say?"

"It's not what you said ... it's what you didn't say!" Gabby said and left.

Melody stood in the middle of her living room, her heart racing with realization. She was, indeed, in love with Zander, just as she thought she was.

CHAPTER 13

ZANDER WAS QUICKLY TOSSING ITEMS into boxes when he heard the familiar sound of gum cracking between teeth. He turned to see Tulu standing in the doorway of the shed. His eyes lit up. He'd always liked her. She was fun and always had grandiose ideas.

"Tulu!" He crossed the room to her, toting his suitcase behind him. "I'd thought by now you'd be in Florida or someplace warm."

"Bria phoned." She closed the door, stopping Zander from leaving. "She told me she was ready to sign the papers and run Sugar Plum." She blew a huge bubble until it popped against her lips. "So, I turned my motorhome right around and came back."

"She should've just signed the papers a few months ago, instead of playing her games." Zander watched as Tulu pulled the gum that was stuck on her lips and shoved it back into her mouth again. He chuckled. He always liked the fact that Tulu chomped on gum. Gum suited her unique personality. "It's good to see you again. How's the open road?"

"A dream, my dear. A pure dream." Tulu waved her arms to the furniture lined up against the wall that Zander designed and built. The bangles on her arms jingled with the swipe of her arms. "I've met the most wonderful people in our big old world," she slapped her hands together.

"Great!" Zander glanced at his watch.

"You're leaving?"

"Yes, Tulu. I'm sorry. I know you loved the idea of Bria and I ... but when she left, everything I knew or thought I wanted crumbled."

"And that includes my niece?" She reached up and started playing with one of her platinum-colored curls.

"Yes."

"Where are you going?" She reached in her coat pocket, pulling out another piece of bubblegum. Unwrapping the pink mound, she added to what she was already chewing.

"I'm not quite sure yet." He grabbed his coat and slipped it on.

"Does it have to do with a certain young lady named Melody?"

"Bria told you?"

"Yep."

"Do you believe in fate, Tulu?"

"It depends, I guess." She cracked her gum a few more times. "Why?"

"Because of Melody. She insisted that she'd made a reservation to stay here, and we aren't even open for business. How can it be? Fate?"

"Perhaps. Who am I to say whether or not it was fate? Maybe it was just an accidental encounter of two people crossing paths. Maybe that's all it was."

"And maybe there's more."

"All I know," Tulu said, tossing Zander a piece of bubblegum, "is that life is sort of like bubblegum."

"How so?" he asked bewildered.

"Well, every now and again life becomes stale, and the way I figure it, you need to unwrap a new piece and add it to what you already have."

Zander walked toward the door and opened it while looking down at the piece of bubblegum he'd caught. "I'll leave my furniture here, for now, but I'll be back for it when I find a place. Please don't let Bria sell my furniture while I'm gone. She never liked that I worked with my hands. I could see her selling everything to spite me. All I know right now is that it's time for me to unwrap a new piece of bubblegum."

"With Melody?"

"Who knows, but ... I have to find out."

"I hope you find what you're looking for."

"You do realize, I am never going to chew this piece of gum. I'll keep it as a reminder of what you just said." Zander smiled, nodded, and left. He tossed his suitcase into the back of his truck with the other boxes he had loaded earlier. Then he waved goodbye and drove away.

Melody lay awake. Her mind wouldn't shut off. It jumped from one conversation to the next, rehashing every word she and Zander had said to each other. Wondering if something else should've been said.

Melody flipped from side to side and sat up, turning the light on next to her bed. Reaching for her laptop, she stacked the pillows behind her for support and leaned back.

She began googling bed and breakfasts in Williamsport. Zander's words danced in her head. "Who are you and what are you doing here? There must be some sort of mistake. You couldn't have made a reservation." Had it really all been a mistake? She knew she'd made the reservation. She'd even entered her credit card number to pay for it. Could it have been the snowstorm causing havoc with the internet? She shook her head while scrolling further down the page. Then she saw it.

She had made reservations at Sugar and Spice Inn in Williamsport. Yet, she had arrived at Sugar Plum Inn in South Williamsport. Melody gasped in horror and jumped from the bed. How could she have made such a mistake? She had never done anything like that before. Ever! She had stayed at the wrong inn. *Oh no*, she thought. *What have I done? He tried to tell me, but I wouldn't listen.* She was such an idiot. Zander had been right all along. She scolded herself while reaching for her phone.

She didn't care that is was three in the morning and that Gabby was sleeping. Melody needed to talk with her now. The phone rang several times, and Melody found herself pacing in front of her bed.

"Melody, what's wrong?" Gabby's voice mumbled through the phone.

"I was at the wrong inn, Gabby!" She practically shouted into the phone. "I spent the weekend with a man who must think I am a complete loon!"

"What? You're not making sense."

"I've been trying to tell you. I didn't have reservations at Sugar Plum Inn. I had them at Sugar and Spice Inn. I ended up in South Williamsport instead of Williamsport." Melody waited for Gabby to reply, but all she heard was her sister laughing. "I don't find this funny at all."

"I do!"

"How did that happen, sis? I've never done anything like that before!"

Gabby laughed even louder. "Oh, Melody," she managed to sputter. "You always were directionally challenged."

"What?" Melody retorted. She was becoming increasingly perturbed. "When?"

"Like the time you got on the turnpike and went in the opposite direction!" Gabby started laughing again. "I mean, who does that, Melody?"

"Just go back to sleep!" Melody abruptly ended the phone call and sat down. She was looking for some empathy from her. Instead, she poked fun of her.

Melody walked to her closet and pulled her suitcase out. Tossing it on the bed, she began aimlessly throwing clothes into it. She was leaving in the morning. She needed to apologize to Zander. She was mortified. If nothing else, she would explain to his fiancée about how she'd ended up at that inn.

CHAPTER 14

THE DRIVE TO WILLIAMSPORT WAS not something Melody was looking forward too. She had egg on her face. Reaching for her travel mug filled with hot chocolate, she took a long sip. It was refreshing on a cold winter's day. The temperatures weren't supposed to get out of the teens all week. At least it wasn't snowing. That is how she got messed up with the inns. It had snowed hard that afternoon, and all she'd seen was the first part of the sign that read Sugar. The rest of it was covered with snow. *So, so stupid.*

She needed to listen to music as she drove. Something to distract her and take her mind off this horrifying faux pas. Switching on the radio, she heard Billy Preston singing "Will It Go Round in Circles." A favorite of hers, and how appropriate. That's what she felt like she was doing. She turned the volume up and started singing along with Billy.

Needing to stretch her legs and refill her mug of hot chocolate, she pulled into Plyer's Buffet-Family Restaurant in Brookville. It was a halfway mark to

Williamsport. Walking in, she set her mug on the counter, requesting a refill as she went to the restroom.

Back at the register, she noticed the woman in front of her looked familiar. She couldn't place her, though. She had platinum hair that was styled in big curls. The woman finished her transaction. As she turned to leave their eyes locked, and she popped a bubble with her gum.

Melody stepped up to the counter and paid her bill. Walking back, she couldn't shake the feeling that she'd seen the woman somewhere before. Where? Unlocking her car door, she tossed her purse on the seat and set her mug in the cup holder.

Then it hit her. A cold chill ran down her spine, and it wasn't because of the temperature outside. She remembered. Slamming her door shut, she rushed through the parking lot, trying to catch up with Tulu. She needed to talk with her. But where had she gone? Melody didn't see her.

The woman with the big curls was the one in the photograph at Sugar Plum Inn. The original owner. Whipping her head around, quickly scanning the parked cars, she spotted Tulu. She was just about to climb into a motorhome.

"Excuse me!" Melody hollered as she ran toward her, "Excuse me! Hello! Wait!"

The gum-chewing woman turned and looked at Melody headed in her direction.

"Please, wait!" Melody yelled again.

"Slow down, honey, before you fall and break your neck," the woman said, putting another piece of gum in her mouth.

Melody caught up with her. Catching her breath, she managed to talk. "I know you!"

"You do?" Tulu asked, cracking her gum.

"Well, kind of. You're the owner of Sugar Plum Inn, aren't you? I've seen your picture hanging in the entry hall."

"Well, goodness. The way you are acting, you'd think I was a famous celebrity or something." She laughed. "I used to be the owner. I signed over the inn to my niece this morning."

"And her fiancée, Zander," Melody softly added, her heart sinking.

"No, honey. Just Bria." Cracking her gum again, she eyed Melody from head to toe. "And who are you?"

"Me?" Melody took a huge breath before continuing. "I made reservations at the inn, but not really. Then I spent the whole weekend alone with Zander. There was this spatula dance and Scrabble and David Muir's-brother-look-alike … and … I love him!"

"Whoa, honey, slow down. I didn't understand a word you just said. Except Zander's name."

"Yes, Zander. I am on my way to see him and tell him that he was right about the reservations."

"Oh honey, he's not there."

Melody's stomach dropped. "What? Where did he go?"

"I don't know, but I have a sneaking suspicion he went looking for you. He left yesterday. If you're Melody, that is."

"I am." Her face washed over with sadness. "But ... he doesn't know my address. How's he going to find me?" Her eyes blinked back tears.

"I'm sorry, Melody."

Melody hung her head in disappointment. She forced a smile in Tulu's direction, quirking her eyebrows. "Thank you. I'm sorry to have bothered you," she murmured as she walked away.

The drive back to her townhouse in Pittsburgh seemed long and drawn out. She dreaded going back home. She wanted so much to see Zander and explain the mix up. But Zander was gone.

CHAPTER 15

MELODY UNLOCKED THE DOOR TO her townhouse to find Gabby feeding the cat. The look on her sister's face was exactly the look she was hoping not to see. The big-sister *I feel sorry for you* look. Melody parked her suitcase by the front door and tossed her coat on top of it.

"Gabby ..." she put her hand up. "I know you mean well, but I'm not in the mood for one of your cheerleader pep talks." Melody scooped up Holly. She was rubbing against her leg and purring. "He's gone, and I have no idea where he is."

Gabby slipped her coat on and smiled. "You look like you lost your best friend, Melody. I'm sorry." She patted her on her arm and left.

"Best friend." Melody looked at Holly while stroking her. "I barely know the man, but ... there was some kind of connection. Now I will never know." She set Holly back on the floor and went into the kitchen.

Noticing the box sitting on top of the table, she laughed at herself. Romance was not going to be a part of her life. She needed to accept that fact and move on.

She'd wasted enough time and energy on those silly notions. She was an adult, not some preteen in love with the idea of being in love. She turned, opening the kitchen drawer. Removing the heart-shaped measuring spoons, she threw them into the box. She'd planned to put the box in the garbage at the end of the week. Before that, she was determined to purge her home of all things heart or anything else that screamed romance.

Zander sat at the far end of the counter at Ritter's Diner in Pittsburgh's Bloomfield neighborhood. He was drinking coffee and tackling a stack of pancakes. The place was busy, and the waitresses were rushing around trying to fill everyone's orders while at the same time topping off his coffee to keep it from cooling off.

He had searched high and low for a phone book. It was completely amazing to him how archaic those had become, along with phone booths. He didn't need a phone to find what he was searching for, just an address that matched the name. Pushing his plate aside while taking another gulp of coffee, he opened the book to the long list of people named Chambers.

He needed a small miracle. If this was indeed fate stepping into his life, along with Melody, then he needed to find her. He didn't have much to go by, just her last name and the fact that she was from Pittsburgh. So, by process of elimination and the luck of finding a pay phone, he had begun calling every Chambers that was listed in the book. He refused to entertain the thought that her number could be unlisted.

He was down to the last three Chamberses that were listed. Pulling out his pen and paper, he wrote the numbers and addresses across it. Was he crazy? Or perhaps out of his head? They'd only spent three days together during a snowstorm. She'd even left the inn without saying goodbye. Considering how the events of the morning went the day she left, he couldn't blame her. Were her apricot lips that tantalizing to him that he would chase her back to Pittsburgh? No, it was more than the color of her lips. She was different. He was hoping she felt the same way.

Paying his bill, he left the diner. He would know by the end of the evening if she felt the same way about him as he did her. She had to be one of these last three people.

It was getting late, but Melody wasn't tired. She tried reading but couldn't concentrate. Her thoughts trailed off the page, leaving the words behind. The sound of her cell phone ringing brought her back. She picked it up off the end table next to her. She looked at the number that was registering. It was Gabby. She swiped the decline button, letting it go into voice mail. Melody wasn't ready to talk with her sister yet.

Across the room she noticed the decorative box where she kept her collection of love letters. She'd been saving them since she was a young girl. Melody and her mother used to go antiquing. That is where she'd fallen in love with love letters, an art form long since forgotten in today's world. With a deep sigh, she snatched up the box and tossed it among the other items on the kitchen table. Glancing around, she decided she was satisfied with what she had put in the box. It was time to throw it away.

She slipped her arms into the lavender sweater she kept by the front door. Taking the box of items with her, she went outside. It was a crisp, cold evening. No one was out at the late hour. The streetlights shone, offering a lighted path to the curb. Normally she wouldn't go out this late, but she wanted to make sure the box went out with the garbage in morning.

She set the box on the curb. Then she turned to go back inside but stopped in her tracks. Someone was standing on the steps leading to her townhouse. She froze. "Who's there?" She called out.

No one answered. She watched as the person set an object on the step next to him. Bending, the person pushed a button, and music echoed into the night. "Just listen," the man said.

Melody took a few steps closer to the stairway. *That voice.* She knew that voice from somewhere. Beginning to climb the steps, she stopped. The music "Valentine" by Martina McBride was encircling her.

The man came closer. Enough for her to see his features.

Melody squealed. "Zander! How did you find me?" The two of them embraced while the song continued. Neither wanting to let go.

"It wasn't easy, that's for sure." He broke the embrace, looking into her eyes. "All I had to go on was your last name and the city where you lived. Do you know how many Chamberses are in the phone book?"

"You didn't!" Melody laughed, covering her mouth with both hands.

"I did!" Zander stopped the music. "I called or went to every address listed. I called the number for this address. A recording came on saying the number was disconnected. I had to try, though. So, I drove here. I had to find out."

Melody burst out laughing. "Oh, Zander! I'm so glad you did. I only use my cell. There's no landline anymore."

Zander's eyes held an intensity that set her toes tingling. "I wasn't going to let you go until I found out if you felt it too."

Her heart jumped into her throat. "What about Bria? I saw the ring on her finger." Just then a few flakes began to fall, teasing her eyelashes.

"Correction: she put the ring on her own finger. She saw it sitting on the mantel."

"But you said you owned the inn?"

"Correction: I never said that. I told you Sugar Plum Inn was not open for business. You insisted that you had made reservations. It was snowing hard. What was I supposed to do? I let you stay." He gave her a boyish grin.

"Oh, yeah, about that ..."

"About what?"

"I didn't have a reservation at your inn. I became flustered with the way it was snowing. I saw the sign to Sugar Plum Inn and *thought* that was where I'd made reservations. It wasn't."

"It wasn't?"

"Um ... no. I had a reservation at Sugar and Spice Inn." She could see his face contorting, trying to hold back from laughing. "I drove back to find you the other day when I realized what I'd done. I wanted to explain. It was too late. You were gone."

Zander's laughter roared, and he pulled her back into his arms. "'My funny valentine' ... then you felt something, too."

"Yes," she whispered as she wrapped her arms tightly around him. "I felt it, too."

ALSO AVAILABLE BY SUSAN MELLON

The Fragrance of Love

The Locket

Look for my next book
Never Too Late for Romance

www.susanmellon.com
susan mellon facebook

If you would like to be added to Susan Mellon's monthly newsletter, message your email address to her on Facebook.

ABOUT THE AUTHOR

Susan Mellon lives northeast of Pittsburgh, Pennsylvania with her husband, Alex. When not writing, Susan enjoys watching movies, vacationing in Walt Disney World, jaunts to New York City, live theater, Pirates baseball and chocolate.

Made in the USA
Lexington, KY
26 November 2019